Case of the MISSING RATTLES

Written by Robyn Supraner
Illustrated by Joan E. Goodman

Troll Associates

Library of Congress Cataloging in Publication Data

Supraner, Robyn.
    Case of the missing rattles.

    (A Troll easy-to-read mystery)
    Summary: Hoping to join Max's new detective
service, Maxine works on his first case of the
missing baby rattles.
    [1. Mystery and detective stories. 2. Lost
and found possessions—Fiction] I. Goodman,
Joan E., ill. II. Title. III. Series: Troll
easy-to-read mystery.
PZ7.S9652Cas   [Fic]   81-10378
ISBN 0-89375-590-7   AACR2
ISBN 0-89375-591-5 (pbk.)

10   9   8   7   6   5   4   3   2

Case of the
MISSING
RATTLES

Max stood on a ladder. He hammered the last nail into his new sign.

BIG MAX—DETECTIVE
No Job Too Small
(Open for Business)

"I want to be a detective, too," said Maxine.

"Sorry," said Max.

"Why can't I?" said Maxine. "Why? Why not?"

"Y is a crooked letter," said Max.

"That's not a reason," said Maxine. "I want a reason!"

"I'll give you four reasons," said Max. "First, you're not old enough. Second, you're too young. Third, you're not big enough. Fourth, you're too small."

"Horsefeathers!" said Maxine. "That's only *one* reason and you know it!"

"One *big* reason," said Max.

"Come on," said Maxine. "You can be Big Max. I'll be Little Max."

"No deal," said Max.

"It's not fair," said Maxine.

Max smiled at her. "Life is not always fair," he said.

Max waited in his office. His notebook was ready. His pencils were sharp. His magnifying glass was polished. All he needed was a customer, just one customer.

He waited and waited. At two
o'clock, someone knocked at his door. It
was Maxine.

"I brought us a customer," she said.

"Wrong," said Max. "Wrong, wrong,
wrong!"

"What's wrong with a customer?"
said Maxine.

"Nothing is wrong with *my*
customer," said Max. "Mine! Not yours!
Now, go away."

"I'll wait outside," said Maxine.

Max closed the door. He pointed to a
chair. "Sit down," he said.

The customer sat down.

Max picked up his notebook. He
picked up a pencil. "What is your name?"
he asked.

"You know my name," said the
customer.

"Just answer the question," said Max.

"Charlie Hobbs," said the customer.
"My name is Charlie Hobbs."

"Where do you live?" asked Max.

"Are you nuts or something?" said Charlie.

Max stared at him.

"I live next door," said Charlie. "Did something fall on your head?"

Max ignored him. He wrote in his notebook. "Okay," he said. "What's your problem?"

"Rattles," said Charlie.

"Snakes?" said Max.

"Baby rattles," said Charlie. "My sister Katy's rattles. They're missing. All of them. I think my mother thinks I took them."

"Did you?" asked Max.

"What would I do with a bunch of baby rattles?" said Charlie.

"Just checking," said Max.

"This is serious," said Charlie. "Will you take the case?"

"I'm busy—" said Max.

Charlie stood up.

"Sit down," said Max. "I'll take the case."

"What do we do first?" asked Charlie.

"Return to the scene of the crime, of course," said Max.

"I'm going, too," said Maxine.

"You're staying home," said Max.

"I'll do as I please," said Maxine. "It's a free country."

When they arrived at the Hobbs'
house, Katy was in her playpen. Her toys
were all over the room. Mrs. Hobbs was
picking them up.

Mittens was barking. She wanted to help. She wagged her tail and picked up Katy's rag doll.

"No! No!" cried Mrs. Hobbs. "Bad Mittens! Naughty dog! Mustn't touch the baby's toys!"

Mittens dropped the doll. She lay down in a corner and put her head on her paws.

"We are here on business," said Charlie.

"We have work to do," said Max.

"We have a mystery to solve," said Maxine.

Max poked her with his elbow. "*I* have a mystery to solve. Get lost!"

"Why don't *you* get lost?" said
Maxine. She sat down next to Mittens.
"*Big,* Big Max!" she said. "What's so
special about being big?"

"I will have to question the suspects,"
said Max.

"What suspects?" asked Charlie.

"Everyone in this house," said Max.

He questioned Katy first. "When did you last see your rattle?"

"Ba ba," said Katy.

"I see," said Max. "Do you remember who was with you at the time?"

"Ga ma doo," said Katy.

"Very interesting," said Max. "Now I have one more question. Think, Katy. I want you to answer truthfully. Do you have any enemies?"

Katy took her time. She looked at Charlie. She looked at Max. "Da da moo pa," she said.

"Thank you, Katy," said Max. "Thank you very much."

"What did she say?" asked Charlie.
"Search me," said Max. "Let's find
another suspect."

Mrs. Hobbs was in the kitchen. "Come in," she said. "Have some milk and cookies."

"Just cookies for me," said Max. "I never drink on the job."

Max ate three cookies. Charlie ate four.

Maxine and Mittens ate the rest.

"Come on, Mittens," said Maxine.
"Let's go for a walk!" She marched out
the back door. Mittens followed her
through a small opening that was a
special door.

Max got on with the questioning. "Tell me, Mrs. Hobbs," he said, "where are Katy's rattles when they aren't lost?"

"In her crib," said Mrs. Hobbs, "in her playpen, on the floor, in her carriage, under the couch . . ."

"I will have to search the house," said
Max.

"Be my guest," said Mrs. Hobbs.

Max looked everyplace. He searched
the attic. He searched the cellar. He
searched everywhere in-between.

"It's no use," he said. "Katy's rattles are not in the house."

"Maybe they fell out of her carriage," said Charlie. "Maybe they're somewhere in the street."

They checked with Mrs. Hobbs.

"Yes," she said. "I took Katy for a walk this morning. We went to the market."

"Did Katy have her rattles?" asked
Max.

"I think so," said Mrs. Hobbs, "but
..."

"That's it, Charlie!" cried Max. "This
is our big break!" He ran out of the house.
Charlie was right behind him.

" . . . but I'm not sure!" Mrs. Hobbs
called after them.

Max and Charlie did not hear her.
They were halfway down the street.
 "Rattle, rattle, who's got the rattle?"
said Charlie.

Charlie found a water pistol.

Max found a "dinosaur."

They both found some money—which
was enough to buy an ice-cream cone.
"Being a detective has its good points,"
said Max.

They walked as far as the market. "Nothing," complained Charlie. "Zero. Zip. Zilch." He leaned against a tower of dog food, when, *crash!* The boxes tumbled down all around him.

"What do Katy's rattles look like?" asked Max, as he helped Charlie pick up the boxes.

"One looks like a lollipop," said Charlie. "One looks like a blue doughnut, and one looks like a little pink bone."

"A bone?" asked Max. "What kind of bone?"

Charlie pointed to a box of dog food. "A bone like that," he said.

"Oh, no!" cried Max. "Let's get going!"

"What's the rush?" asked Charlie.

"I'll explain when we get home," said
Max. He started to run.

Charlie ran, too.

Katy was on the floor. "Ga doo ma ma," she said when she saw Charlie and Max. She waved something that looked like a little pink bone. In her other hand was a blue doughnut.

Maxine was there, too. She was
holding something. She shook it. It made
a rattling sound. It looked like a lollipop.
Only it wasn't.

"You're a little late," she said. "Sorry,
Charlie. Sorry about that, Max!"

"How?" said Max.

"Where?" said Charlie.

"Simple," said Maxine. "I followed Mittens. She showed me where she buried them in the garden."

"She thought they were her bones," said Max.

"Wrong," said Maxine. "Wrong, wrong, wrong! Mittens felt left out. She wanted some attention. She took the rattles so someone would notice her. Everyone needs attention, Max. Even people who are younger than other people. Even puppies."

Mittens barked.

"Okay," said Max, "I get the message."

"I was hoping you would," said Maxine.